The Little Angel

The Little Angel
A Story of Old Rio
By Alice Dalgliesh

Illustrated by
Katherine Milhous

1947
Charles Scribner's Sons
New York

TO THE CHILDREN WHO READ THIS BOOK

You will enjoy the story of The Little Angel more if you know just a little about the history of our friendly neighbor, Brazil.

After explorers came across the ocean, Brazil belonged to Portugal. The King of Portugal also reigned over the big colony across the Atlantic. Then Napoleon Bonaparte conquered most of Europe, including Portugal, and the members of the Portuguese Royal Family fled to Brazil.

This made Brazil the center of the Portuguese Empire. At the time when this story begins, in 1819, Dom João was King of Portugal (in exile) and Regent of Brazil. His son, Dom Pedro, had come with his father to Brazil, and had married an Austrian princess. A little daughter was born to Dom Pedro in 1819, and Rio was glad to welcome a little Princess born on Brazilian soil. In 1822 Dom Pedro became the Emperor of Brazil, when that country declared its independence from Portugal.

We know Rio today as a handsome, modern city, with wide streets, fine homes and tall apartment houses. It is interesting to look back to the days when it was a picturesque red-roofed Portuguese colonial town with narrow streets, teeming with people in the varied costumes of the period.

At the court of Brazil there was a French painter named Jean Baptiste Debret. He was there to paint everything that was going on in the country, and he was very thorough about it. He made three big books of pictures which showed not only court scenes and festivals, but the people of Brazil, the streets of Rio, and the church festivals. He wrote descriptions of them, too. There are very few of these big books in libraries, but if you should see them you would know exactly how Brazil looked in the days of the Emperors. It was in these books—and others—that the artist and I found the little angel and the material for this story and its pictures. The end papers of the book are photographs of drawings of old Rio by Debret himself; and the artist has purposely drawn some of the figures in her pictures almost as they are in Debret's books.

✳   ✳   ✳

You will notice how important Saint Anthony, or Santo Antonio, is in the story. He was the household saint in Brazil, and one time he was said to have saved Bahia, in northern Brazil, from the Dutch, who were trying to capture it. The Procession of St. Anthony took place on Ash Wednesday, not on the fête day of the Saint.

There are only a few Brazilian words used in this book, most of them are names that the family and slaves used for Maria da Gloria. If they called her *Mariazinha* that meant "little Maria." *Papagaiozinho* meant "little parrot" and *Anginho* "little Angel." *Menina* is "little girl" and the nurse calls her *Sinházinha* which means "little senhorita" or "little mistress."

Contents

CHAPTER I.

The Family of Senhor Silva

SENHOR Paulo da Silva was proud of his family. On Sundays when they went, all together, to the public Promenade, Senhor Silva walked first. The others followed in line, according to age, the youngest children first, and the slaves last of all. Every once in a while, Senhor Silva would look back proudly and say to himself,

"There is no finer family in all Rio."

It was not such a large family as families went in old Brazil, but it was a handsome one. No, it was not such a large family, only

Senhor Silva, who was growing a trifle stout,

Senhora Silva, who was pleasantly plump,

Maria Luiza, who was as pretty as any little girl in Rio,

Roberto, who was lively and frequently disobedient,

Paulo and Pedro, one thin, one round and fat,

Miguel, who was only a baby and who was carried in Carlota's arms,

Carlota, who had been nurse to all the babies, and the other slaves, Thereza and Rosa, José, Domingos and Antão.

1

Just as Senhor Silva had decided what a fine family it was, trouble would begin. First of all there would be a slight scuffling, then the scuffling would grow louder and louder. Senhor Silva, knowing quite well what the disturbance was, would march on, pretending not to notice. After a time, as the noise grew, he would stop, face the line and roar,

"Pedro, Paulo, are you fighting for place again? It is absurd and ridiculous, for everyone knows that Paulo is almost a year younger than Pedro and must walk *before*, not *after* him."

Then the scuffling stopped and Pedro slipped back into place behind Paulo. All the family looked serious except Maria Luiza who giggled a little, for she was not in the least afraid of her father, even when he was being most impressive.

There were great advantages to being the only girl in the family, but Maria Luiza was thoroughly tired of it. More than anything in the world, she wanted a sister. Every day she prayed to Santo Antonio for one, and so far, the saint had not answered her prayers.

Maria Luiza thought it over as she walked demurely along in sight of Papai's important coat-tails. When she wanted anything very much she did not only *ask* Papai for it, she coaxed him. Perhaps Santo Antonio needed a little coaxing. She must try that and see what would happen.

The scuffling had begun again. Pedro and Paulo were once more involved in argument. Papai's voice roared out,

"Pedro, Paulo—"

Maria Luiza sighed. It was very tiresome to have four brothers and no sister. She really must do something about it. The very next day she would do it.

Now they were at the Promenade. It was a pleasant place, with its shady avenues of mango and bread-fruit trees. The sea lapped against the stone wall, making gentle little sounds. Everyone was happy except Papai and he was sniffing the air as he always did, and complaining of the odors. Mamae tried to soothe him but knew in her heart that Papai was always bent on improvement, and that even in Heaven he would complain that the golden streets were not kept clean.

"It's a disgrace," Papai was saying. "We have the most beautiful harbor in the world, yet everything is thrown into the Bay. There's no excuse for it, ha?"

This happened every time they went to the Promenade!

CHAPTER II.

A Garland for a Saint

IT was a sweet-smelling morning. With the sun newly risen and the dew still on grass and branch, the fragrance of jasmin came lazily in through the shuttered windows. And suddenly Maria Luiza awoke.

The night had been hot and Maria's hair hung damply in long, straight strings. She pushed it back impatiently with a hand that also was warm and moist. But now there was a cool freshness in the morning air. Maria Luiza sat up and took deep breaths of it. Before the day grew hot, before the rest of the household were up, she must carry out her plan.

So she jumped out of bed and wriggled her moist little body into a dress. Although she put on only the one garment, this was an effort, for Maria was not accustomed to dressing herself; Carlota was always there to help her. Quietly, in her bare feet, she crept downstairs and out into the garden.

On a branch of the magnolia tree a green parrot swung upside down and eyed Maria with delight.

"Louro, louro!" he called, swinging round and round, catching the branch with claws and beak. Then in a louder tone, "Maria! Ma-ri-a!"

4

"Hush, silly one," said Maria Luiza. "You will wake Mamae and she will want to know what I am doing."

The parrot stopped swinging, ceased its shrill talk and watched Maria as she went about the garden, picking flowers that pleased her especially. Starry sweet jasmin, the little pink hearts of the coral vine, the delicate blue blossoms of the jacarandà, the flaunting scarlet of hibiscus; Maria Luiza put them all in the skirt of her dress. She was not alone in the garden. Already the bright colored humming birds were darting to and fro, sampling the nectar on the flowers with their long bills.

Maria looked at them thoughtfully. It must be delightful to be a "kiss-flower," with not a worry in the world except the gathering of honey. She sighed as she sat down on the edge of the pool and began to arrange her flowers. Carefully tying their stems together with bits of still-dewy grass, she wove them into a sort of garland. The parrot swung himself down from the tree, sidled across the grass and pulled at the flowers in Maria's lap.

"Foolish bird!" Maria Luiza said affectionately, scratching the bird's red top-knot. "Can't you see that I am busy?"

The white ducks that lived in the pool swam up to Maria, begging for food. She tossed them some jasmin petals; the ducks pecked at them halfheartedly.

"Later I shall feed you," Maria assured them. "But now I have no time."

The ducks swam away, disappointed. Then, her work finished, Maria rose, shook the fallen petals from her lap, and hung the garland about her neck. The warm wind had dried her hair and it blew in soft tendrils against her face. There was no one but the parrot and the ducks to see how lovely she looked with her small olive-colored face framed in bright flowers. Maria herself could see the picture as she looked down into the pool, but it did not occur to her that she was pretty. Such thoughts would come later, as she grew older. Turning away from the pool, Maria walked over to look out at the world through the bars of the iron gate.

It was a lovely world that she saw. The Silva house was on a hill overlooking the beautiful harbor. Rio de Janeiro in the early nineteenth century was a fair-sized city, its red-roofed houses clustered on the hill or straggling down to the water's edge. The sun shone on the dancing water of the bay and on the little islands that dotted it like green jewels. In the distance, clouds were gathering around the Organ Mountains, but a single peak lifted itself from the clouds. Maria Luiza shivered a little as she saw it. Sometimes the Finger of God was wholly friendly, but at other times, when Maria was doing wrong, it could look so threatening! Though, Maria argued to herself, it need not threaten her now, for she wasn't doing wrong, only keeping a secret all to herself.

PAPAI

PEDRO . PAULO . ROBERTO . MA

ANTÃO

JOSÉ

DOMINGOS

ROSA

~ARLOTA ~ MIGUEL

JIZA ~ MAMAE ~ THEREZA

She looked up at the funny, friendly stone lions that sat on each gate-post as if guarding the house. Paulo had named them, and he took the greatest care of them. Once he had even climbed up on the gate to give each stone lion a bone!

Suddenly the quiet of the garden was broken by shouts and the patter of bare feet. Maria's brothers came running into the garden and splashed noisily into the pool. The ducks tried frantically to swim out of reach. Roberto grabbed at them and one white feather remained in his hand. The ducks quacked indignantly, and the drake, who had lost the beautiful curl in his tail, preened himself hastily. The parrot, back in the magnolia tree, shrieked with delight, for he had never cared much about those white birds with their solemn ways.

The boys splashed joyously in the pool, drops of water glistening on their brown bodies. All at once they saw their sister.

"Maria! Maria Luiza! What are you doing here so early?"

Maria stood looking her brothers over critically. They were tiresome at times, but she loved them. Especially she loved funny, fat, little Paulo who was too fond of *doces* (sweets) and good things to eat.

Roberto, always the one to tease, pointed a finger at her. "Your hair isn't combed and your dress is on all crooked."

Maria's tender feelings left her. "What I am doing here is my own affair," she said. "At least I am not pulling the tail feathers out of helpless birds."

Roberto stuck the feather defiantly behind his ear and flopped up and down in the water.

"Quack, quack, quack! Maria's cross! Maria's cross!"

Maria knew there was no chance of getting the better of him. So she straightened the garland around her shoulders and hurried through the garden door. In the wall of the courtyard around which the house was built there was a niche, and in this niche stood the household saint, with the Holy Child in his arms. Maria reached up carefully and hung the garland of flowers around the saint's neck. Then she dropped to her knees and prayed:

"Blessed Santo Antonio, bring me a little sister, not a brother, already the house is too full of those, but a sister, a little sister I can play with. Please, blessed Santo Antonio."

CHAPTER III.

Sins—Big and Little

THE day was going badly in the Silva household, for the Senhora was having one of her spells of being furious with all the slaves.

"Lazy good-for-nothings," she scolded. "My life is a misery. Servants are not what they were when I was a girl. Two hours ago that José went to market and he is not back yet. The cook is asking for the fowl for soup and where is it—where is it, I ask you? Where?"

Domingos, who was sweeping the courtyard, stirred himself as the angry words whirled around him. José was always late, one could expect that, but today he had gone a little too far with it. One hour perhaps—but *two!* Now when he, Domingos, went to market he was always back on time, but that was the difference between him and José. José could take a tongue-lashing from the Senhora, peace-loving Domingos could not.

"Let me go and see what is keeping him, Senhora," he suggested mildly.

Senhora Silva hesitated. Without José work went slowly, without both José and Domingos it would stop entirely. But there was the chicken—and the soup. It would soon be time for the midday dinner and there would be nothing for them to eat. So she nodded.

"Very well, Domingos, but if you are not back soon—"

Domingos dropped his broom and hurried off. Rosa, who was watering the flowers in a languid way, looked up at her mistress.

"I could go," she suggested mildly. "Perhaps Domingos will not know where to find him."

"No—no—no!" scolded the Senhora. "Everyone knows that you are making eyes at José. If I should send you he would forget all about the time—he would *never* come home. Ah, here he is. José, where have you been? Two hours, it is a disgrace."

The hot waves of her anger beat against José but he gave no signs at all of noticing them. A tall, handsome Negro, he smiled up at his mistress, showing all his white teeth.

"The market was crowded, Senhora. The men had not come in from the country with their fowls. When they came, so many wanted them. I waited until there was a good choice. You would not want me to buy little old fowls, Senhora? Little old thin fowls? Little old *sick* fowls?"

José held up the three chickens as he spoke, they squawked dismally. "See, they are such beautiful birds, well worth waiting for."

"Well, then, take them to the kitchen—and *hurry*,"

said the Senhora in a calmer tone. José went off with speed, followed by Rosa, smiling to herself. He was so clever that José, thought Rosa, always he knew how to get the better of the Senhora.

The soup was ready and giving out the most appetizing smell when the boys, who had been out with their tutor, came home. They were full of what they had seen.

"Down by the market, when we passed," said Roberto "there was a puppet show. The man had the figures on his hand and they spoke in such squeaky voices."

"But I know how they spoke," said Paulo. "The man spoke for them, I peeped behind the curtain."

"Ah," said their mother. "Now perhaps I know why José took so long to buy his fowls. It would, I think, be almost better always to send Domingos to the market. He is not easily distracted."

"I wish I had seen the puppet show," sighed Maria Luiza, when they were out in the courtyard after the meal. "You boys have all the fun. Why do I have to be a girl and always stay at home?"

"A girl," said Roberto with a wise air, "is not meant to have fun. She is only good to stay at home and sew and say prayers—and maybe some day get married."

"But I hate to sew—and I don't want to get married —or—or—or say prayers—" spluttered Maria indignantly.

"Sh!" warned Roberto. "Father Sebastian!"

The children rose as Father Sebastian came into the

room. Tall, with a kindly face and eyes through which shone a sort of inner light, he was their mother's confessor. The children all loved him and not one of them would have done the least thing to hurt his feelings. Maria hoped he had not heard her remark about prayers, for she was a devout little girl and had not meant what she said. A deeper, guilty feeling suddenly came over her. That—oh, that was much worse, in fact it was almost wicked. What if Father Sebastian should know about it?

Father Sebastian sat down and Paulo climbed on his knee.

"Paulo," said the Father sternly, putting a finger on Paulo's round fat tummy, "you are, I believe, fatter than ever. Those *doces*—"

Paulo wriggled uncomfortably. "I have given up *doces*," he said.

"And how long ago?"

"As long ago as—as—as yesterday."

Father Sebastian laughed. "Then I can scarcely as yet expect an improvement in your figure," he said. "And about the others? Any small sins to report?" Each week he conducted an informal confessional for the children, who did not in the least mind telling him their "small sins."

"No," said Paulo.

"No," said Pedro.

"Roberto?"

Roberto hung his head. "I do not know how big a sin it was," he said. "I pulled the cat's tail and it scratched me." He held up his hand on which a long red scratch stood out clearly.

"Which would seem to indicate that the cat took care of *that* sin," said Father Sebastian.

"And—I pulled a feather from the duck's tail—"

"Which the duck could not take care of," said Father Sebastian. He turned aside to hide a smile, for sometimes he found it hard to be serious over the small sins. "It is your one fault, Roberto, this teasing—teasing—and the little care you have for those of God's creatures who are weaker than you."

Roberto shifted from one foot to the other.

"Sit down," said the Father, "and I will tell you a story of a good man who lived in Brazil and who never forgot that every creature that flies and crawls and walks has feelings and can suffer pain."

The children gathered around eagerly, for if there was one thing they loved, it was the stories that Father Sebastian told.

"It happened in Brazil, many years ago," he began. "In the jungle there was a little hut with a thatched roof and in it lived a good man named Father Anchieta. All day long he worked, and always for the good of others. Never a moment did he have for his own pleasures. In the day-time he taught the Indians to read and to sing beautiful

songs to the glory of Our Lord and Our Lady. In the nighttime he sat by the light of a candle writing—writing—writing so that his pupils might have books to read.

"But it was not only the Indians who knew the great kindness of Father Anchieta. All the feathered folk of the jungle, and the beasts of prey—yes, even the poisonous serpents that crawled among the fallen leaves—were his friends. It is said that when the days were hot the birds gathered, and spreading their wings, formed a canopy over the good man's head to keep off the burning rays of the sun. The puma and the jaguar were his companions as he journeyed through the forest. Once when he had been away from his hut and returned, his companions were amazed to see, walking on each side of him, a beautiful puma. As he neared the hut the animals turned and went back into the jungle."

The children were quiet for a moment. The walls of the room seemed to have melted away and they walked in the jungle with Father Anchieta. Then, with a start, they came back to reality.

"I will try to think about the—about the creatures and how they have feelings," said Roberto.

"I will not eat so many *doces*," said Paulo, vaguely aware that the occasion called for some sort of promise, whether it had any connection with Father Anchieta or not.

From the courtyard came a high-pitched Negro voice,

one very familiar to the children—and always welcome, for the owner of it carried a tray of the sticky sweets that were Paulo's undoing.

"Cry *meninos*, cry *meninas*

Papai has money in plenty.

Come buy, *meninos*, come buy."

Paulo was the first at the door, followed by the other two boys. Maria and Father Sebastian were alone in the room.

The priest smiled and shook his head. "So go the good intentions!"

"But I am glad the boys have gone," said Maria. "For I have a sin to confess and it is not a little sin, Father."

Father Sebastian looked startled. "Not a small sin, *minha filha*? Is it possible?"

Maria nodded. "I did something dreadful. I prayed to Santo Antonio for a little sister and he did not send me one. So I made him a beautiful wreath of flowers and I prayed again, and he did not send me one. So—" Maria's voice trailed off into silence.

"So," said Father Sebastian encouragingly. "So you punished Santo Antonio. Is that it?"

Maria's large brown eyes seemed to fill her whole face. "How did you know?"

"It was easy to guess. What did you do?"

"First," said Maria, "I stood him in water up to his neck. Nothing happened."

"And then—"

"And then—" Maria's voice was nothing but a whisper. "Then I threw him out of the window into the garden."

Father Sebastian looked down at her with a very serious expression.

"That was neither kind nor devout," he said. "And did you leave him in the garden?"

"That is what makes the sin so bad." Maria's voice could scarcely be heard now. "I—can't find him!"

For a moment Father Sebastian did not know what to say. He had not expected such things from gentle Maria Luiza. Roberto—yes—but not Maria Luiza.

"Daughter," he said at last, "*minha filha*—we must go into the garden and find the saint."

"But I have looked everywhere," sighed Maria. "And he is not there."

They had by this time reached the edge of the pool.

"Did you look in the water?" asked the Father.

"No—" said Maria doubtfully. "But he couldn't be there. I threw him in the flower bed, where it was soft— and sweet smelling."

"Very thoughtful of you, to be sure," said Father Sebastian coldly. "But he happens to be in the water, because I can see him there." He pushed back the sleeve of his cassock, plunged his hand into the water—and there was Santo Antonio, his colors brighter than ever, the Holy Child still in his arms.

"I do not know how he got there," drooped Maria. "Unless Roberto—"

"Be responsible only for yourself," said the priest gently. "And now, put the saint back in his niche and ask Our Blessed Lord to forgive you for your sin."

"Indeed I will," said Maria thankfully.

As they went back to the courtyard, the boys came to meet them, cheeks bulging with *doces*. A black cat came across the courtyard waving her tail. She was a cat without personality but she was later to be the mother of the kitten Gatinho, who would make up for all his mother lacked. As the cat came near, Roberto stretched out his hand, drew it back, and instead went nearer to her, talking in soothing tones.

"*Miss, miss, miss!*" he called. "*Miss, miss, miss!* Come, *miss*," he said. "I will be Father Anchieta in the jungle and you will be the puma and walk behind me—so."

But the cat, remembering the past, spat fiercely and retired to a corner where she glared at Roberto. From the doorway Father Sebastian laughed softly.

"Sometimes," he said, "I wonder what life would be like without children. If Santo Antonio is kind there may soon be another small one in this household."

CHAPTER IV.

A Double Birthday

THE days went by and the weeks and the months. Every morning Maria Luiza prayed to Santo Antonio, and always she treated him with respect. One morning she wakened early and lay, half asleep, listening to the bells. How they clanged and called to each other from one end of Rio to another! There came the deep voices of the Candeleria bell and of São Bento. Above them sounded the shrill voice of São José and the bells of Santa Rita and Santa Thereza.

Carlota came into the room and now Maria Luiza was wide awake.

"Why do the bells make so much noise, Carlota?"

"With good reason *Sinházinha*," answered the nurse, "because a little princess is born. Dom Pedro has a daughter. Why is it a girl? It should be a boy, some day to rule over Brazil."

Then Carlota waited a minute and added words that made Maria Luiza sit bolt upright in bed.

"And the same day has brought a little girl to this house. You have a sister, *Sinházinha*."

"Santo Antonio heard my prayer!" chattered Maria

Luiza. "May I see her, Carlota? Please, Carlota, when may I see her? When?"

"All in good time," said Carlota. "She has been with us only a few hours. After all, she is very new from Heaven and who knows, if you frightened her, she might fly back to live among the angels."

"But I want to see her before she quite loses her wings," laughed Maria. "Please, Carlota."

They called the baby Maria da Gloria, because that was the name given to the little Princess. She was christened on the same day as the Princess, when the streets were hung with flags and flowers.

It seemed as if all Rio was glad to welcome the royal baby and all the other little Marias who had been born on the same day—or almost on the same day. There were fair-haired Marias, dark-haired ones, cream-colored and black and brown. In a tiny house on the edge of the town a Negro mother bent over her baby and murmured her name—Maria da Gloria. The baby's hands curled around her finger, curled and uncurled and the mother kissed the palms that were almost white—as a very small Negro baby's are. "Your hands are more beautiful than those of the Princess," she said.

The day had really been Carlota's. For it was Carlota who rode proudly in the sedan chair, carrying the baby, while the rest of the family walked! Carlota in her finest and gayest costume, jangling with bracelets and hung about by strings of colored beads. José and Domingos, who carried the chair, grumbled very softly, though loud enough for Carlota to hear.

"That we should have to carry *her!*"

"She is growing fat!"

"And heavy—*how* she is heavy!"

But Carlota sat like an ebony queen, her bright skirts spread around her, the baby in her arms, pretending not to hear their mutterings.

It was Carlota who held the baby as the priest gave her the name that fell like music in the still air of the incense-laden church—"Maria da Gloria—Mary of Glory."

It was Carlota who tied the string of charms around the baby's neck to keep off evil spirits.

The feast that came after the christening was something to remember. Maria Luiza's mouth watered long afterwards as she thought of it, and Paulo ate so many *doces* that he had a pain in his stomach. There was always a feast for a new baby in Rio, but Maria da Gloria's was special, for she shared a royal birthday.

"We must invite all our friends to see what a lovely baby she is," said Senhora Silva proudly. "She is much prettier than Dom Pedro's baby, I am sure of that." And she wasn't far wrong, for the royal baby was not a beautiful child. She was fair and blue-eyed, like her mother who had been an Austrian princess. But little

Maria da Gloria da Silva was dark-eyed, a true child of
Brazil.

The christening feast was held in the garden, where
the fountain splashed softly in the pool, the ferns were
cool and damp. The long pink trails of the coral vine
almost hid the stone wall and hibiscus held its scarlet
flowers like flags. The guests gathered, talking, embracing
one another, congratulating the parents. Everywhere
among the trees and flowers there were small tables with
all kinds of good things to eat, and plates piled high with
sweets. From the jacarandà tree the green parrot swung
down, worked his way up the leg of a table, helped himself to a sweet, and was up the tree again before he was
even noticed. Pretty, flighty Rosa, whose duty it was to
wave a brush over the food and keep off the flies, saw him
but was too lazy to drive him away. Too lazy and too
busy keeping an eye on José, who came and went with
trays of food.

The chatter and the laughter was continuous. Suddenly it stopped, there was a strange breathlessness in the
air—and Carlota came into the garden. The bundle of
lace in her arms stirred a little, gave a sudden, wailing cry.

"Hush then, *menina*," said Carlota, jiggling the baby
violently up and down. The guests gathered around making appreciative sounds—once in a while one could hear
a few words. "The sweet one!" "So much hair!" "So
beautiful." "The very image of her mother."

Maria Luiza caught the last words and stood on tiptoe to look carefully at the baby sister. Somehow the funny little pink morsel didn't look much like her pretty, plump mother. It wasn't important whom she looked like—she was Maria Luiza's sister and she was here—that was all that mattered.

CHAPTER V.

"Viva o Brasil!"

THE delight of having a little sister grew day by day. Maria da Gloria was, so Carlota said, the best natured of all the Silva babies. She did not mind in the least if Maria Luiza treated her as if she were a big doll, or if her brothers played noisily around her. The days slipped by with pleasant family doings and special events. There were days special only in the Silva household, the day when Maria da Gloria cut her first tooth, the day she took her first step. And there were other special days, the festivals that brought color and music to Rio and filled the night sky with starry showers of rockets. They dotted the calendar of the year, these days, as the jewelled islands sprinkled the Bay. But there was one day that stood out above them all, a day the children would never forget.

One morning when Maria da Gloria was three years old, Carlota had taken the baby into the garden and Maria Luiza was there, too, for she seldom let Maria da Gloria out of her sight. The parrot did not swing down from a branch to greet them, he stayed where he was and eyed them with bright, questioning eyes. Since the baby had come no one had paid so much attention to *him*.

26

"Maria—Ma-ria," the parrot tried experimentally, but Maria, as usual, was too busy with the baby to notice him. So the parrot swung himself up to a higher branch, ruffled up his feathers and sulked. The ducks came quacking to ask for food, but Maria did not even notice them.

Carlota sat on a bench, her bright skirts spread like the petals of a flower, the baby on her knees. Little Maria blinked in the sunlight, laughed and held out her hands to a blue butterfly that flew lazily just out of her reach.

"She likes the color," said Maria Luiza, kneeling beside Carlota so that she could see the baby. Her back was turned to the house, so she did not notice that her father and brothers had come out into the garden or that they stood there in silence, looking at her. Carlota's surprised expression made her turn around; and somehow she knew that her father had brought important news.

"Pa-pai!" said little Maria, holding out her arms. And, although it was evident that Senhor Silva was seething with excitement, he could not resist her. So, taking the baby from Carlota, he held her on one arm and looked down at the children. They waited, breathlessly, to know what he would tell them.

"Maria Luiza," he began in the most important voice that he kept mysteriously tucked away most of the time and only brought out for special announcements. "Roberto—"

"*Linda!*" chortled Maria da Gloria, reaching for the

butterfly, which was hovering almost within reach.
"Pretty!"

This was disturbing and quite spoiled the Senhor's important speech. Frowning, he handed his small daughter
back to Carlota and tried again.

"Children! This is an important day for Brazil and
for Brazilians. We are now a free people!"

The children listened politely but quietly, not being
quite sure what Papai meant. Seeing their puzzled faces,
he went on.

"No longer are we to be told what to do by those across
the sea. Portugal cannot make our laws. Dom Pedro has
proclaimed the freedom of Brazil. He is now our Emperor."

The children were quite silent for a few minutes. The
older ones knew what this meant to their father and how
he had hoped—and worked—for a free Brazil.

The silence was broken by Maria da Gloria's clear little
voice.

"*Linda!*" she said. This time the remark seemed slightly
more appropriate. Everyone laughed, the children hugged
their father, Roberto, fired by patriotic enthusiasm,
swung himself up on the iron gate, balanced himself pre-
cariously by holding on to a stone lion and shouted:

"Viva o Brasil! Viva Dom Pedro!"

The children cheered and shouted with him. "Viva o
Brasil!" Maria da Gloria clapped her hands, the parrot

joined in with shrill screams, the ducks quacked loudly. Nothing, not even the fireworks and processions that came later, at the coronation of the Emperor, seemed as joyous to Maria Luiza as did this first family celebration. No, not even the day when the children went with Papai to see the Royal Family appear on the balcony of the Palace, and little Princess Dona Maria da Gloria smiled directly at them. That was a day to remember, but always the clearest picture of Brazil's first Independence Day would be of Roberto clinging to the stone lion and shouting, "Viva o Brasil!"

When the excitement had died down and Papai had gone into the house, taking the older boys with him, Maria Luiza and Miguel sat on the grass near Carlota.

"Carlota," said Maria Luiza, "tell us how Dom Pedro came to our country?"

Carlota grinned delightedly. It was a story that she loved to tell, but one that the children asked for all too seldom. They usually preferred the story of the Monkey and the Armadillo, or another of the lively folk tales that Carlota had brought from her home near the Amazon River.

She lost no time beginning the story, but today it was told without details and without embroidery, for Maria Luiza kept her to the point.

"It was when I was only a girl," began Carlota in her soft, deep voice. "I was living in Bahia then, my mother belonged to your grandmother's household. Ah! It was a lovely town, Bahia—"

"About Dom Pedro, not Bahia," politely suggested Maria, who knew how easily Carlota could go into long descriptions of her beloved town.

"I remember it as yesterday," Carlota went on. "I well remember that morning when the ships came into the Bay. I could see them from the top of the hill, and everyone was crowding and laughing and saying, "It is the Queen —and the Prince Regent and his family. They are here!"

"Did they come ashore at once?" asked Maria Luiza, who liked this part of the story.

Carlota laughed so that her necklaces jingled and the baby in her lap jounced up and down.

"No, *Sinházinha*, that was what was so amusing. They ran so fast from Portugal that they left most of their clothes behind! And they had to wait on the ship to borrow clothes to come ashore! But everyone was glad to lend their best. I remember that your grandmother lent a petticoat to the Queen—and how proud she was. A beautiful petticoat, *Sinházinha*, with lace—"

"I know about the petticoat," nodded Maria Luiza. "The Queen was crazy, wasn't she, Carlota?"

"A little queer in the head," admitted Carlota. "But the little princes and princesses were so sweet no one cared if the old lady was not quite in her right mind. Dom Pedro, he was a little boy, then, with his pretty curly hair, looking around him with big eyes so full of surprise."

"And then he came to Rio, and now he is Emperor," said Maria Luiza, with a sigh of content. Maria da Gloria, you must say 'Viva Dom Pedro!' "

But Maria da Gloria had, as always, to say things in her own way.

"*Linda!*" she said, trying to catch a sunbeam that flickered across Carlota's face. "*Linda!*"

CHAPTER VI.

Growing Up

IT SEEMED no time at all until Maria da Gloria was six and Maria Luiza fifteen. Maria Luiza grew taller and lovelier every day. As for Maria da Gloria, she was such a lively little creature, with so much impishness shining out of her dark eyes, that one really could not say whether she were going to be a beauty or not. Each member of the family had a different nickname for her. Papai called her *papagaiozinho*, little parrot, because she chattered from morning until night. Maria Luiza, remembering the morning when she had hoped to see her small sister's wings, called her *anginho*, little angel. The boys mostly called her "little pest," but said it with affection.

There were other babies in the house now, but they were not Silva babies. Rosa, grown more sedate and perhaps a little less lazy, was married to José and it was her two dark babies who sprawled on the floor. On this particular day, Rosa herself was sewing a dress for Maria da Gloria. Senhora Silva and Maria Luiza sat on the couch, feet tucked under them, and sewed. On a low stool, Maria da Gloria bent over her reading lesson. There was silence except for the sound of the fly brush, now worked by a younger slave, and Maria da Gloria's reading. Her clear little voice rose and fell in a curious chant as she read A B C D E F G, or her numbers, *um, dois, tres, quatro,* or proudly spelled out a few words.

"There, I can read the whole page!" she announced triumphantly. "Now can I see my dress?" She jumped off the stool dropping her paper on the floor, where the babies scrambled for it. Rosa snatched it from them, giving each a sharp spank on his plump and naked rear.

"It's quite wonderful!" sighed Senhora Silva. "Quite wonderful, this education. In my day a girl wasn't allowed to read or to write. Nothing but prayers—and more prayers—and things she must know to keep her house when she married. Talking of marriage, Maria Luiza—"

"Yes, Mamae?"

"I want to see my new dress," interrupted Maria da Gloria wriggling with impatience. "Rosa, show me my new dress?"

Rosa held up the dress and Maria da Gloria clapped her hands.

"It is beautiful! Next Sunday I shall wear it."

Senhora Silva looked up from her sewing, looked Maria da Gloria over critically.

"You think too much of your appearance," she said a little coldly. "A girl should always be modest, and you, Mariazinha, are no more nor less than a little peacock."

608567

"But Mamae," said Maria da Gloria in a voice of honey, "Papai says that I am almost exactly as you were when you were a little girl."

Lula, fascinated by Maria da Gloria's boldness, leaned forward so as not to miss a word, forgetting her duties, so that the fly brush hung motionless in the air. There was a joyous buzzing as the flies gathered for the assault. Six of them lit on Senhora Silva's hand at once. She shook them off angrily, motioned to Lula.

"Are you asleep, girl? Always dreaming—of what? Servants are not what they were when I was younger, they are a constant torture and a misery. How would you like it, girl, if I should—sell—you—"

Lula came to herself with a start, the fly brush moved briskly, the flies, discouraged, flew on to the farthest wall.

"As I was saying," the Senhora went on, "a girl should be—"

"Married," said Maria Luiza hastily. "You were speaking of marriage, Mamae."

"So I was," said her mother, whose somewhat vague mind was easily distracted. "I was saying, Maria Luiza, that you are now fifteen and it is time to be thinking of marriage."

"If you say so, Mamae," murmured Maria Luiza dutifully. "And if Papai—"

"Papai has already made arrangements for you," said Mamae. "You will see." She rose as she spoke and went

out of the room. Maria Luiza rose too and walked out as
if in a dream, with Maria da Gloria pattering anxiously
after her. Maria Luiza went to her own room and stood
at the window looking out into the garden. Maria da
Gloria came up quietly and slipped her hand into her
sister's.

"Maria . . . who is this man you are going to marry?"

"I don't know," said Maria Luiza in a strange, tight
voice. "I don't know, *anginho*. Papai has chosen."

Maria da Gloria persisted. "What do you want him to
look like?"

Maria Luiza frowned and considered. "He should be
tall and dark—and young—" Her eyes went to a picture
on the wall. It was a picture of Dom Pedro, Emperor of
Brazil, a slender young man with dark, curling hair and
romantic dark eyes. "But I have no choice."

"You could pray to Santo Antonio," suggested Maria
da Gloria helpfully. "I am going to pray to him to send
me a sister."

"A sister?" puzzled Maria Luiza. "Why a sister?"

"Because I am going to lose you," answered Maria da
Gloria quickly. "And you know how you prayed to Santo
Antonio for *me*."

"So I did, Mariazinha," Maria Luiza's hand closed
tightly over her sister's small one. Somehow she had not
thought that, if she married, Maria da Gloria would *not*
be a part of the new home. It came over her suddenly that

none of them would be, not Papai, not Mamae, not Roberto or Pedro or Paulo or darling little Miguel. There would be only herself and this perfectly strange man that she had not even seen. Putting her cheek down on Maria da Gloria's dark hair, Maria Luiza burst into tears.

It would have been a very sad time indeed if Paulo had not suddenly appeared. Paulo was nine now, and a good deal thinner. He still loved all creeping and crawling things as well as everything that flew or went on four legs. One never knew what kind of pet Paulo might bring home. The last had been a monkey, an exceedingly mischievous one that soon left for another home.

This time, as she saw Paulo, Maria da Gloria gave a little scream. Maria Luiza looked up, and through her tears she saw an astonishing sight. For there, on Paulo's arm was a long, green object. It was something like the little lizards that darted to and fro on the garden wall, but *much*, much larger. It looked at the girls solemnly, with jewel-like eyes.

"Paulo! Whatever is that?"

"It is my iguana," said Paulo, stroking the lizard's horny back.

"Where did you get it? The horrid creature," said Maria da Gloria.

"It's *not* a horrid creature. Domingos found it in the market and he bought it for me. A man brought it down from the Amazon. See, it's quite tame."

"Mamae will not like it," shivered Maria Luiza, her tears suddenly forgotten.

"Gatinho will not like it," added Maria da Gloria. Gatinho was her kitten. The whole family had tried to find a name for the lively ball of fur but there were so many differences of opinion that finally the kitten was simply called Gatinho, "little cat."

"It does not matter what Gatinho likes or does not like," announced Paulo. "And *my* pet will have a name that *is* a name. I shall call him Geraldo. And if that little-cat-without-any-real-name spits at Geraldo, he will find out —well, he will find *out*."

CHAPTER VII.

Maria Luiza Refuses

"LOOK, Maria Luiza, he is coming!" Maria da Gloria almost fell over the balcony in her excitement. "Your husband is coming!"

"He isn't my husband," said Maria Luiza, who was indoors, in front of the mirror. One must look one's best when the man one might marry came to visit. She tucked a fresh white rose into her hair and stood back to admire the effect.

"But he will be! Come quick, Maria Luiza—oh, you're too late! He's gone in at the door."

"What did he look like?" asked Maria Luiza trying not to sound too interested. "Was he tall? Was he short—fat—thin?"

"I didn't really see," confessed Maria da Gloria. "He was in a hammock—the slaves carried him—and there were other slaves. But I think—I think he was tall and thin."

Maria Luiza nodded approvingly. "He has made a journey because he lives on a *fazenda*—oh, not so far, but too far to walk. Papai says it is a beautiful farm with a big house—and lots and lots of servants and trees—and flowers. You may come and visit me there, little sister."

40

Maria da Gloria giggled. "To think of you having a house and lots of servants, Maria! It's very funny."

"I don't know why," Maria Luiza tossed her head. "After all, I'm fifteen." But even as she spoke, she looked very much like a little girl.

"You must come with me when I go down, *anginho*. I am afraid to go alone."

Maria da Gloria pouted. "He doesn't want to see *me*, only you. But I will go," she added, for she was full, brimming over, almost bursting with curiosity. "And I shall take Gatinho," she added, picking up the kitten. "He will want to see, too."

Carlota appeared in the doorway. "Hurry, *Sinhazinha*, your father and—and the Senhor are waiting in the garden." She stood and watched as the two girls went downstairs together, and there were tears in her eyes, for Maria Luiza was her first baby—and now her first baby was a woman and thinking of marriage. Carlota felt suddenly old and tired.

Senhor Silva and his guest sat at a table in the garden drinking small cups of coffee. The parrot watched them suspiciously from his perch in the magnolia tree. If they would turn their heads for a moment, he would take the chance to go down onto the table and help himself to a beakful of sugar. He did not like the tall, thin man who talked so eagerly, because, as he talked, he fixed the parrot with his keen black eyes.

There was a slight rustle. Senhor Silva's guest turned, and, framed in tall greenery, he saw the two Marias. They stood there for several minutes, saying nothing. The thin gentleman, meanwhile did not fail to notice how beautiful the elder sister was, or to admire the rose in her dark hair.

"Come, child," said Senhor Silva impatiently—but Maria Luiza hesitated.

"Maria—"

At that moment Gatinho took matters into his small furry paws. Jumping down from Maria da Gloria's arms, he pranced sideways across the grass in the direction of the visiting Senhor. Arching his back in a friendly way, he rubbed against the Senhor's legs.

"Maria—"

But Maria Luiza, watching Gatinho, paid no attention at all to her father. The kitten rubbed and purred, then, annoyed and astonished at not being kindly received, reached upwards and sank his claws into the Senhor's leg.

There was a squawk of anguish from that important gentleman, then, very suddenly indeed, a hand reached down and Gatinho found himself flying through the air. Never had he traveled so rapidly! It was fortunate that he traveled in the direction of his little mistress, who caught him and held him close to her indignant bosom.

"Maria—" it was Senhor Silva's voice again.

But, with the swiftness of light, Maria was gone. Up the stairs she went, a small violent tornado, threw herself

on her bed and cried until her whole body shook with the sobs. Mamae came in, Carlota, Rosa, Maria da Gloria, they all gathered around her, concerned, comforting.

"What is it, Maria? Did Papai—"

"N-no," sobbed Maria Luiza. "Not Papai—"

"Then what—tell us—"

At that moment Senhor Silva came storming up the stairs.

"Maria Luiza! That I should be disgraced by my daughter. Ready for marriage, she is, and she runs away like a silly little girl. Runs away as if the devil himself were after her."

Maria Luiza sat up. Her eyes were red, her cheeks streaked, her nose swollen and puffy, but she managed somehow to summon up a great deal of dignity.

"I will not marry him," she said clearly. "He is old and he is bald and I do not like him. From the top of his bald head to his too-tight shoes, I do not like him. And he was cruel to Gatinho."

Papai stormed again. "He is wealthy."

"That does not matter," said Maria Luiza firmly. "He is old and bald and his shoes are tight and he is cruel and I will not marry him."

Papai could not have been more surprised if Gatinho had turned and bitten him. Was this his gentle, tractable, oldest daughter? Maria Luiza, who always did as she was told? Besides, Brazilian daughters did not tell their fathers whom they would or would not marry. It simply wasn't done.

Senhor Silva was so surprised that he stood there not knowing what to say next. His wife pushed him firmly out of the room.

"Go, Paulo. You can do nothing when the child is so excited. Wait until she is calm."

The news spread through the house, seething, boiling like lava from a volcano.

"She will not marry the Senhor!"

"She says he is old."

"And bald!"

"And cruel!"

"No, she will not marry him."

"She has defied her father!"

In the kitchen, Antão put so much pepper in the soup that he himself sneezed. Rosa scolded and clucked sympathetically. Carlota paced the floor and wrung her hands. Senhora da Silva waited for her daughter to be calm so that she might reason with her.

But, excited or calm, all that Maria Luiza would say was, "I will not marry him. He is old and bald and he is not kind."

"My daughter is not well—is not herself today. Senhor Silva told his guest. "We must arrange another meeting."

So the thin gentleman with the bald head rode back to his *fazenda* in his hammock, a little ruffled, a little bewildered, wondering what it was all about. He was not a very intelligent man, and, being a very wealthy one, he could not imagine that any girl in Rio would not be pleased to marry him.

"She is very pretty," he said as the hammock swung with the rhythm of the slaves' walk. "She will be a great addition to my home. But I hope—yes, indeed, I hope she is not delicate. That would never do. I must think this over, no?"

But he found that, after all, the decision was not to be his. Senhor Silva loved his daughters very much, and he had not been pleased by Gatinho's unwilling flight across the garden. So, for a time, Maria da Gloria kept her sister, and there was no further need to ask Santo Antonio for a new one.

CHAPTER VIII.

Battle of the Lemons

THE days of the Lenten season were coming, and before them the Carnival that turned Rio into the gayest, maddest place imaginable. The whole Silva household was in a state of turmoil. The boys planned their carnival costumes, Maria Luiza talked of parties, the slaves also made their carnival plans and did no work at all. Only Maria da Gloria seemed a little apart from the general excitement. For, this year, what was the carnival to her? It was Ash Wednesday—the day *after* the carnival—that would be her Day of Days. For on that day she was to have an honor for which every little girl in Rio dreamed and hoped.

Father Sebastian had given her the news one day after he had finished telling the children a story. Drawing her against his knee and tilting her face up with one hand, he looked down into her brown eyes.

"Little Maria," he said. "How would it seem to you to be, this year, an angel in the Procession of Santo Antonio?"

An angel! She, Maria da Gloria, an angel! And to walk in the procession with Father Sebastian! She swallowed hard and tried to say something, but could not.

"So?" questioned the Father. "You do not want to be an angel, no?"

"Oh, I do—I *do*," stammered Maria da Gloria. "I have prayed every night that I might be chosen."

"And now you are!" smiled Father Sebastian. "I have talked with Mamae about your costume. Pink—I think it will be—or blue—or is yellow more to your liking?"

"Yellow," murmured Maria da Gloria dreamily. She could already see herself in the beautiful angel dress. From that moment a carnival costume held no charm at all for Maria da Gloria. At least not until the actual days came, and then even Maria da Gloria could not help being excited by the costumed figures in the streets, the haunting rhythms of the *carnaval* songs, the music of the primitive instruments by which the songs were accompanied.

Then there was the Battle of the Lemons! That was the greatest fun of all. For now the families came out on the balconies of their houses and joined in the throwing of waxen lemons filled with scented water. What matter if one's clothes were soaked through? One simply retired for a few minutes and came back in fresh clothes, which in a few minutes were as wet as if one had just come out of the bath. Laughter filled the air, and the soft plop plop of lemons. Maria da Gloria shrieked with joy as one hit Roberto square on the cheek and spattered all over him, filling the air with perfume.

"Oh, look!" shouted Paulo. "Look—in the street! The Senhor!" The children looked and broke into gales of laughter. For there, among all the lemon-throwers in the street was one staid citizen who, to protect himself, had raised his umbrella. This was a delight to the small boys and a regular shower of lemons fell on the umbrella.

"Why," said Roberto, "it is the Senhor who wished to marry you, Maria Luiza! What is he doing on foot? Perhaps you had better go down and rescue him?"

Maria Luiza tossed her head. "I hear he is visiting at the home of Marianne," she said. "And I wish her joy of him and his old umbrella. The man I marry must be able to throw a lemon and laugh as he gets one back. Mariazinha —careful!"

Maria da Gloria did not have time to dodge the lemon that was coming her way from a balcony across the street. It hit her on the shoulder, broke in a dozen pieces over Gatinho, who was in her arms. Startled and annoyed, Gatinho spat at the strong-smelling liquid that drenched his fur, leaped from the arms of his little mistress, and disappeared indoors.

Paulo laughed. "Poor Gatinho! He takes his lemon no better than the Senhor!"

The fun went on, fast and furious. But when the battle was over and the children went back into the house, Gatinho was not to be found. They searched everywhere, and soon Maria da Gloria was in tears. Her voice trembled as she peered into cupboards and under beds calling "miss, miss, miss" to a kitten that never came.

"The *carnaval* has frightened my Gatinho away," she sobbed. "I shall never see him again."

"Cats always come back, don't cry, little parrot," soothed her father.

"But kittens may not come back. Gatinho is only a kitten and he won't know how to find his way home."

The tears continued to flow, and that night, as Maria da Gloria lay in bed, listening to the sounds of the last of the carnival, she prayed under her breath,

"Blessed Santo Antonio, who takes care of little lost things, Gatinho is a very little thing and he is lost. Help me to find him."

The prayer seemed to bring comfort, and with the tears still on her lashes, Maria da Gloria fell asleep.

In the morning she awakened with no more tears, but a quiet confidence that on this day she would find her kitten. It was a quiet morning, for everyone was exhausted by carnival festivities, and it was the first day of the Lenten season. Left much to herself, Maria da Gloria began to wonder about Gatinho.

Perhaps, she thought, Gatinho was coming back. Perhaps he was even now just outside the house, mewing pitifully, asking to come in. She *must* go and see.

So, quietly, Maria da Gloria slipped out of the big door into the street. Up the street she looked, and down. Gatinho was not there.

A tall *quitandeira* selling *doces* came swinging by.

"Cry *meninos*, cry *meninas*,
Papai has money in plenty.
Come buy, *menina*, come buy."

Her voice was soft and full and pleading. The *doces* in her tray were pink and sugary, but today the sight of them had no charm for Maria da Gloria. She shook her head.

"Perhaps," she said to herself. "Perhaps Gatinho is just around the corner. The streets look alike, he may be mixed up. I shall go and see."

So Maria went just around the corner and there was no fluffy kitten waiting for her. Just around another corner, and another. Now it was Maria da Gloria who was confused, who found that the streets looked all alike.

"I think," she said firmly, not allowing herself to be frightened, "this is the way home. I am sure I came down this little street. Then there is just one more turn and then—our house." So, bravely, Maria started up the little street, not knowing that every step was taking her farther and farther from home.

CHAPTER IX.

In the Streets of Rio

AT FIRST there were not many people. In the district near Maria da Gloria's home nearly everyone was sleeping late after the carnival. But as she wandered farther from home and came nearer to the center of the city, the streets were full of people and of noise. Maria was a bewildered little girl, indeed.

Not too bewildered, however, to be interested in all the strange sights and sounds and smells. More than once Maria wrinkled her pretty nose as a particularly strong smell crept into it. The sights she tucked away in her mind in a long string, like the shining silver beads of a necklace.

There were Negro women in the gay dress of Bahia, and there were many *quitanderos* with their wares. Along the street were open-faced shops selling all kinds of goods. A plump man drowsed in the doorway of his shop and Maria thought she would ask him if he had seen Gatinho.

"Please," she said—the man awoke with a start—"did you see a little white kitten go by?"

The man shook his head and promptly went to sleep again. Maria da Gloria went on. Six Negro men pulling a cart on which were large crates of coffee seemed to take most of the street; they were singing so loudly that Maria decided it would not do to ask them if they had seen her kitten. So many people and all so busy, how could they notice one small kitten?

A last she saw someone who did not seem to be particularly busy. A well-dressed man was standing near the wall of a house, he seemed to be doing nothing at all.

"Please Senhor, have you seen a white kitten—" began Maria. The man frowned and pretended not to hear her. Then, very quietly, a window above him opened and a hand stole out. In the hand was a red rose and it fell at the man's feet. Maria sighed. That was why he couldn't answer her. She knew Romance when she saw it.

Oh! but she was tired! The strange sights and colors began to blur as tears came into her eyes. She wanted Gatinho, but more than that she wanted Mamae—and Papai—and Maria Luiza—and the safe, comfortable walls of her own home. Not even the sight of the doorway puppet show that her brothers had seen comforted her. The puppets danced and sang, a puppet lover kissed the hand of his puppet lady, but Maria saw none of it.

Then along the street came something that made her feel even worse. It was the funeral of a little Negro baby, a flower-bedecked funeral that somehow, under its pink blossoms, held all the sadness in the world. The people who walked with the funeral were singing, a wailing

chant. The tears that had been in Maria's eyes overflowed and ran down her cheeks.

"What is the trouble, little one?" asked a voice, so kind that Maria was surprised, for by this time she was thoroughly sorry for herself and convinced that there was not a single kind person in all the streets of Rio.

"I am lost," sobbed Maria. "I only meant to go just around the corner from my house to look for my kitten, and then I went a little farther and I could not find the way home."

"And where is home?" asked the stranger. Maria could not see exactly what he looked like, because her eyes were too full of tears, but she knew that he was tall and young.

"It is a white house and it is on the hill, and there are little streets that go down to the water. And we have a big magnolia tree in the garden," said Maria helpfully.

"Hm," said the stranger. "And you don't know the name of the street?"

"No," said Maria, feeling small and foolish. Papai had not taught her the name of the street because, after all, no one expected a little girl to go out into the streets of Rio and get lost.

"Then we must start all over again," said the stranger. "What is your name, *meninha?*"

"Maria da Gloria da Silva," answered Maria promptly. She knew *that*.

"Silva!" said the tall young man. "I know the name. Is your father by any chance a friend of Monsieur Debret, the painter?"

"Oh, yes!" smiled Maria da Gloria. "Oh, yes! Monsieur Debret comes often to our house. Why, he made a picture of us one day—of Mamae and Maria Luiza and me." The tears cleared from her eyes and she could see that the tall young stranger was handsome, with dark eyes and black curling hair. Strangely enough, he looked a little like the picture of Dom Pedro that hung in Maria Luiza's room. An idea came into Maria's head, and she smiled and dimpled.

"If you will take me home, my family will be so happy," she said.

"Very well," said the young man. "I am a pupil of Monsieur Debret, and I shall be happy to meet your family. But let us find out where you live, Senhorita Maria da Gloria."

Smiling again at being called Senhorita, Maria da Gloria slipped her hand into the stranger's. "Ask someone where my father lives," she said.

Senhor Silva, being in government service, was well known, and there was more than one person to tell where the white house on the hill could be found. Maria da Gloria trotted happily along beside the young man, and soon they turned into the little street that was familiar.

"There it is! There is my house," said Maria.

Going into the courtyard, the young man clapped his hands.

"*Quem é?*" asked a lazy voice. "Who is there?"

"José!" cried Maria. "I am home!"

"And a good thing," grumbled José. "For the last hour this house has been a crazy place."

The voices had been heard and Senhora Silva and Maria Luiza appeared at the top of the stairs.

"Mariazinha! How you frightened us!"

Maria Luiza ran down the stairs and threw her arms around her sister. Then she looked up at the tall young man who had brought little Maria home. He was looking down at her admiringly, and something in his face told Maria da Gloria that things were going well—very well.

CHAPTER X.

The Little Angel

WHEN the first joy over the return of Maria da Gloria had died down, everyone suddenly remembered that she would have to be an angel in the procession in a very short time indeed. So Carlota and Maria Luiza, Rosa and Senhora Silva became very busy all at once. Maria da Gloria, a bit weary and footsore from her travels, enjoyed the attention. First she was washed and powdered and curled and scented. Then at last came the wonderful angel costume with its stiffened skirts, its curious halo, its tiny wings. The elaborate headdress of flowers and ribbons was placed on Maria da Gloria's curls. Last came the necklaces, the bracelets, the rings, the earrings.

Now the family stood back to admire. Very little of Maria da Gloria could be seen under all the jewels and decorations, but Carlota noticed that her child's face was pale and there were circles under her eyes. There should have been a smile of complete happiness on Maria da Gloria's face but instead her head nodded and her mouth opened in a wide yawn.

"I think—I am—sleepy—" she announced.

There was general consternation and a good deal of fluttering and whispering.

"She has walked too far!"

"She is tired!"

"She can't go to sleep *now*."

"We must keep her awake."

"I am sleepy," said Maria da Gloria with another large yawn, "and my feet hurt me. I am going to sit down."

"You can't sit down!" Maria Luiza's voice rose to a squeak, it was so full of anxiety. "You can't sit down in that dress, Maria da Gloria!"

Tears came into little Maria's eyes and no one knows what might have happened had not a clapping of hands in the courtyard announced that visitors were arriving.

In came Senhora Silva's sister, bringing with her Maria da Gloria's two cousins, one a year older, one younger. It had been arranged that the cousins were to meet at the Silva house, from where they would go by carriage to join the procession.

In they came in their glittering costumes, Maria Thereza and Maria Francisca. Sheer curiosity to see if the costumes were lovelier than hers made Maria da Gloria forget that she wanted to sit down and wanted to sleep. Jealously the little girls fingered each other's silks and jewels, sniffed each other's fragrance, and each privately decided that she was the most charming angel of all. But aloud they said:

"How lovely you look, Maria da Gloria."

"Not lovelier than you, Maria Thereza."

The boys trouped in to see. Tall Roberto dropped to one knee and kissed his small sister's hand with mock solemnity.

"I salute you, Princess," he said.

"I am an angel," said Maria da Gloria stiffly, at which all the brothers laughed.

"For today only," said Roberto.

Miguel came no farther than the doorway where he stood, quite overcome by so much feminine beauty and brilliance.

Senhora Silva clucked like a mother hen gathering her brood.

"Come, children, it is time to go. Come, Maria Thereza, come, Maria Francisca. Maria da Gloria, do not on any account go to sleep. And you *must* not sit down. All of you will have to stand in the carriage, though how you will all get in I do not know." She continued her chatter as she shepherded the angels to the top of the staircase.

In the courtyard José and Domingos, waiting by the carriage, looked up to see what seemed to be the heavenly host descending the staircase. For one moment the three little angels made a charming picture on the stairs, then, suddenly, there were three shrill screams and the angels clung to each other frantically.

"It will bite me! Take it away!" shrilled Maria Thereza.

"It is going to eat me," wept Maria Francisca, the tears making little rivulets on her powdered cheeks.

Senhora Silva and Maria Luiza rushed to the rescue. "It is only Geraldo," said Maria da Gloria calmly.

And there, on the lowest step, was Geraldo, the iguana, his long green body stretched entirely across the step, his head slightly raised, fixing the terrified angels with his bright eyes.

"Paulo!" called Senhora Silva. "It is that iguana again. TAKE HIM AWAY!"

When the green creature had been tenderly collected by Paulo, and the angels' tears had been dried and cheeks repowdered, the heavenly band once more made its way towards the carriage.

"And waste no time coming back, José, Domingos," called the Senhora. "We will be ready when you come. For the older members of the family would watch the procession from the balcony of the house belonging to the mother and father of Maria Francisca; the Silva house not being on the route.

The angels were lifted into the carriage by José and Domingos. Carlota went with them. With a clatter of hoofs and a scraping of wheels the carriage drove out— very carefully so as not to upset the little girls who, because of the stiffness of their dresses, had, indeed, to stand.

Senhora Silva sank into a chair and fanned herself violently.

"Paulo," she called, "come here. I want to speak to you."

Paulo came in, kissed his mother's hand.

"What do you want of me, Mamae?"

"It is that iguana," said Senhora Silva. "You cannot bring him in the house, Paulo. After this he must stay in the garden."

"Just because he frightened the girls?" protested Paulo.

"No, not because of that. Is it possible that you did not hear Papai when he got up this morning?"

"I did hear him," admitted Paulo. "He was bellowing like a bull. But I did not know what was the trouble."

"The trouble," said Senhora Silva, "was that iguana. Do you know where he was?"

"Under the bed?" suggested Paulo.

"Worse than that. There on Papai's pillow he was, asleep, with all the length of that green body stretched out."

Paulo laughed; he could not help it.

"I wish I had seen Papai! But, Mamae, I will try to keep Geraldo in the garden. I promise! After all, Papai was not too pleased the morning he found Gatinho on his pillow. He does not like *things* on his pillow."

"Gatinho!" sighed Senhora Silva. "I had almost forgotten him!"

CHAPTER XI.

Procession of Santo Antonio

THE Silva family assembled on the balcony of Tia Maria Jesus's house to watch the procession go by. They were all there, Mamae, Papai, Tia Maria Jesus, Maria Luiza, Roberto, Pedro, Paulo and Miguel. Carlota was there, too, for she could not miss seeing her baby in the procession. Only Gatinho was not present, and no one could imagine where *he* was.

The day was warm, and the procession seemed to be a long time coming. The boys leaned over the rail, idly watching the people in the street, and their talk was not of the procession but of Gatinho.

"It does not seem possible that he can have gone far," said Pedro.

"A kitten surely cannot walk very far, can he?" asked Paulo.

"Gatinho was a very *strong* kitten," sighed Miguel.

"I think," said Roberto, "if Papai will permit us, we will go, after the procession is over, to look for Gatinho. For, if he is not found, Maria da Gloria will cry again."

"That would be too bad," agreed Paulo. "She should be happy, not sad on the day that she is an angel."

64

"We will see to it that she is not sad," said Roberto firmly. "If we *all* look for the kitten we are bound to find him."

"Boys!" warned Senhora Silva. "The procession is coming. We must watch for our little angel."

The first part of the long procession was coming down the street. Soon it was under the balcony. The boys and Maria Luiza leaned forward eagerly. Carlota's necklaces and earrings jingled and jangled with excitement.

What a procession it was! First came a small, proud angel led by a priest and scattering rose petals as she walked. Behind her were more angels in pink and blue and yellow. Then came the first platform, flanked on each side by men bearing tall, lighted candles.

"Ah!" sighed Carlota. "It is beautiful." It was always beautiful, though she had seen it many, many times.

On the first platform stood two large figures, a king and queen. The next float was Santo Antonio's own, and there he stood, carrying a small cross of gilded wood. Beside him was a figure of Christ in a silken robe, and He, too, was bearing a cross. Tableau followed tableau. Angels followed angels and still there was no sign of Maria da Gloria. As another tableau came in sight, Carlota jangled so that the Silvas were sure this must be their particular angel. They leaned forward eagerly, but the angels were still strange, and the platform held a Negro Saint Benedict. As this one passed, the slaves at the sides of the street fell to their knees, for this was their very own saint.

"My kinsman!" breathed Carlota proudly and then, "My baby!"

For in front of the next tableau walked a little angel in yellow, and Father Sebastian held her by the hand. Maria da Gloria walked before the platform that held an image of Our Lady, surrounded by clouds of silver gauze among which were heads of cherubs. Proudly Maria walked, but, as she passed the balcony, Father Sebastian said a word to her and Maria looked up, gave her family a shy, fleeting smile, then dropped her eyes again and returned to her angelic dignity.

"She is as lovely as a real angel," said Carlota.

"But she looks sad," sighed Maria Luiza. "She has not forgotten her kitten."

"But that is quite all right," assured Roberto, "because *we* are going to find him."

The procession went on up the street towards the Convent of Santo Antonio. Maria da Gloria yawned, her feet tripped a little. Father Sebastian looked down at her.

"It is only a short way, now, little Maria. And then you will see the thousand candles burning at the shrine of Santo Antonio."

Maria da Gloria looked up and smiled bravely. Her feet were sore, her eyelids very, very heavy. Suddenly she held the Father's hand more tightly.

"Father! It is Gatinho!"

There, by the side of the procession was a small, be-
draggled, frightened kitten. Maria da Gloria broke from
the procession for a moment, gathered up the dirty little
object, was back again holding Father Sebastian's hand.

Father Sebastian was embarrassed. An angel with a
kitten? That would never do. He took the kitten gently
from Maria and concealed it in his wide sleeve. Gatinho,
full of ungratefulness, scratched him more than once.
Father Sebastian winced but held tightly to Maria's
hand. He longed to shake the kitten out of his sleeve,
but that would not do, either.

On and on went the procession, and heavier and heavier
grew Maria's eyelids. The road was long, the hill steep.

They were at the steps of the Convent of Santo Antonio when the small head with its heavy crown of flowers
nodded—nodded—

Father Sebastian, seeing that his little angel was truly
falling asleep on her feet, leaned down and picked her
up. With a sleepy angel on one arm, a kitten in his
sleeve, the good Father was not exactly comfortable,
but he bore it nobly. Up the steps he went and into the
chapel where the thousand candles burned and the air
was heavy with incense.

Maria da Gloria opened her eyes for one fleeting second.

"The thousand candles—" she murmured drowsily,
"they are bright. Gatinho—Santo Antonio—" and Maria
da Gloria fell asleep.

CHAPTER XII.

The End of the Day

SO, once again, Maria da Gloria was brought home to the white house with the big magnolia tree in the garden. This time she was carried, for she was still fast asleep, her head on Father Sebastian's shoulder. It was a good thing that the Father was not fat, for he had to walk a long way, and Maria da Gloria grew heavier every minute.

It was with a sigh of relief that the Father handed his burden over to Carlota, shook the kitten out of his sleeve, and examined the long red scratches on his arm.

"If you did not belong to little Maria, your neck would not be safe," he told the kitten. Gatinho, delighted to be home, pranced sideways across the courtyard, his tail held stiffly erect. Maria da Gloria stirred slightly in Carlota's arms.

"Gatinho?"

"He is safe, child," soothed Carlota, and carried her baby into the house. Father Sebastian followed, with one fierce, backward look at the prancing Gatinho. Somehow he had forgotten all about Father Anchieta and his kindness to all dumb animals.

That evening was Santo Antonio's own. Although it
was not his feast day, Maria da Gloria said that he had
brought them so much happiness that they would make
the evening his. Soon the saint was entirely surrounded
by flowers, and by candles that made a soft glow in the
dark courtyard. The last of the candles was placed by a
young man with black, curling hair who had come to
pay his respects to—oh, of course, to Santo Antonio.
Maria Luiza presented him, very gravely and properly, to
her father.

"Papai, this is the Senhor who found our little angel
and brought her home."

"We have much to thank you for," said Senhor Silva,
embracing the young man cordially. "You are, so my wife
tells me, a pupil of my good friend, Debret. Any friend
of his is welcome in this house."

The flickering light of the candles fell on Maria Luiza.
The young man looked down at her and smiled. Gatinho
came prancing across the courtyard and rubbed against
the young man's legs. He picked the kitten up and
stroked its fur. Gatinho settled happily against him,
purring loud approval.

From the gallery above, Maria da Gloria, watching,
gave a sigh of relief.

"He is not old and he is not bald and his shoes are not
too tight and he is kind to Gatinho," she whispered to
herself. "I think he will be Maria Luiza's husband." Maria

da Gloria was so full of content that she did not even protest when Carlota came to carry her off to bed.

"It has been a good day, Carlota," she sighed, her arm around Carlota's neck.

"A good day, *Sinházinha*," echoed Carlota's deep, full voice. "A good day, indeed."